Yasmin
the Night Owl
Fairy

by Daisy Meadows

ORCHARD

The Twilight Fairies' magical powers
Bring harmony to the night-time hours.
But now their magic belongs to me,
And I'll cause chaos, you shall see!

Sunset, moonlight and starlight too,
There'll be no more sweet dreams for you,
From evening dusk to morning light
I am the master of the night!

Contents

Contents

Night or Day?

"Hold on tight, Rachel," Kirsty called to her best friend, Rachel Walker. "We're almost there!"

"I'm right behind you, Kirsty!" Rachel called back.

The girls were walking carefully across the wobbly bridge that was strung between two trees in the Forest Fun adventure playground.

The bridge was made of wooden slats with sturdy rope handles. It swayed and wobbled gently from side to side and up and down as the girls moved across it, making them shriek with laughter.

"Oh, this is just the *best* fun!" Kirsty gasped. "I love Camp Stargaze, Rachel. There's so much to do here."

The girls and their parents were spending a week of the summer holidays at Camp Stargaze, and the Forest Fun playground was in a clearing in the woods just outside the camp. There was a treetop walk, several wildlife hides and two zip slides next to each other, as well as the wobbly bridge. The biggest tree in the clearing, the one the girls were heading to along the wobbly bridge, had a wooden treehouse in its branches.

There was also a twisty slide wrapped around the tree's trunk that led down into an underground house

under the roots of the tree. It was late afternoon, just after tea-time, and the girls were still enjoying the warmth of the summer sunshine.

"I know," Rachel agreed. "Camp Stargaze is brilliant. And not only that, we're in the middle of another exciting fairy adventure, too!"

When Rachel and Kirsty had arrived at the camp, their fairy friends had asked for their help once more.

The girls had met the Twilight Fairies who were responsible for making sure that the hours between dusk and dawn were peaceful and harmonious in the human as well as the fairy worlds, with the help of their special bags of magical fairy dust. But while the Twilight Fairies were at a party under the stars, Jack Frost and his goblins had stolen the magic bags from the fairies! Jack Frost was determined to cause night-time chaos and so, with his icy magic, he'd sent the goblins to hide the bags away in the human world. But Rachel, Kirsty and the Twilight Fairies had already found four of the seven bags, and they were hoping to find the others, too.

"Rachel, Kirsty!" a voice shouted. "We're over here."

The girls glanced up and saw their new friends, Matt and Lucas, hanging out of one of the treehouse windows. Rachel

and Kirsty wobbled their way to the end of the bridge and went to join them inside the treehouse.

"Have you been on the zip slides yet?" Lucas asked with a grin.

Kirsty shook her head. "I think I need to recover from the wobbly bridge, first!" she replied.

Matt was still hanging out of the window. "Look, Lucas," he said, pointing down at the ground below them. "There's your mum and Lizzy."

Lucas's mum and his little sister were wandering through the clearing. They waved up at the treehouse, and Lucas, Rachel, Kirsty and Matt waved back.

"Let's go down the twisty slide and say a proper hello!" Rachel suggested.

The top of the silver slide was just outside the treehouse door. Rachel climbed onto it and then immediately shot downwards with a shriek of surprise.

"It's really slippery!" she cried as she disappeared from view.

"Watch out, Rachel!" Kirsty yelled as she too jumped onto the slide. "Here I come!"

14

Laughing, Rachel whizzed around the trunk of the tree and then through the door of the underground house at the bottom of the tree. She tumbled off the end of the slide and onto a soft mat. Kirsty came flying into the underground house a few seconds later, and the two girls grinned at each other.

"Here come the boys!" Rachel remarked as they heard Matt and Lucas sliding towards them.

First Matt, and then Lucas, whizzed down into the underground house. Then all four of them climbed out and ran to join Lucas's mum and Lizzy. They were staring very intently at a large, leafy bush.

"What are you looking at?" Lucas asked curiously.

"Hedgehogs," Lucas's mum replied, her and Lizzy's eyes wide with delight. "Look!"

Rachel and Kirsty peered into the bottom of the bush, and saw two small hedgehogs scampering around among the leaves.

"Aren't they cute?" said Rachel as the hedgehogs scurried busily to and fro. Just then Kirsty heard a rustling noise in the undergrowth behind them. She spun round and caught a glimpse of grey fur and a black and white striped head. Quickly she nudged Rachel.

"There's a badger over there!" Kirsty whispered.

Rachel, Lucas and the others watched in amazement as the badger came into view. He was snuffling through the leaves in search of something to eat.

"This is great!" Matt said, looking very excited as the badger hurried past, taking no notice of them. "I've never seen a badger or a hedgehog in daylight before."

Kirsty frowned. "Matt's right," she said to Rachel. "Don't hedgehogs and badgers usually come out at night?"

"Let's go up to the wildlife hide in the treetops and look for more animals," Rachel suggested.

"We're going back to the camp to play football," Lucas told the girls. "See you later."

The wildlife hide was concealed behind

a canopy of leaves in the branches of one of the trees. Kirsty and Rachel climbed the ladder and then hurried along one of the wooden walkways

that connected the treetop trail. When they arrived, the hide was empty. There were wildlife posters on the walls and two pairs of binoculars lay on the seat in front of the viewing window.

"Look, Rachel, we can see right across the camp," Kirsty pointed out, picking up a pair of the binoculars.

"And beyond the camp, too," Rachel added. She took the other binoculars and peered through them. "We can see the river we sailed up to get to the camp on the day we arrived. And I can see cows and sheep in the field across the river – OH!"

Kirsty looked startled.

"What is it?" she asked.

"The farm animals are all fast asleep!"
Rachel told her. "Isn't that strange?"

Kirsty trained her binoculars on the
field across the river. Now she too could
see that the cows and sheep were all
sleeping contentedly!

"But it's still day-time!" Kirsty pointed out, puzzled. "Why are the night-time creatures like the badger and hedgehogs awake during the day, and why are the animals like the cows and sheep, who *should* be awake, asleep?"

Magical Owl

"Do you think this could be something
to do with Jack Frost stealing the Twilight
Fairies' magic dust?" Rachel suggested,
looking worried.

"It *must* be!" Kirsty went on with a
frown. "After all, everything's been going
wrong at night-time since Jack Frost and
his goblins stole the magical bags."

"But it *isn't* night-time," Rachel said, "The sun's still shining, and it's not even dusk yet!"

The girls exchanged confused glances. But suddenly a soft, hooting sound outside the hide made them both almost jump out of their skin.

"What's that noise?" Kirsty exclaimed nervously.

"I think it might be an owl," Rachel suggested. "And it sounds like it's close by. Let's go and take a look."

The girls crept out of the hide. They could still hear the gentle *whoo-whoo* sound and they followed it along one of the walkways towards the treehouse. Suddenly Kirsty clutched Rachel's arm.

"Look!" she whispered, "There, on that big branch near the roof of the

24

treehouse!"

Rachel looked where Kirsty was pointing and her face lit up with delight. A nest had been built in the crook of the branch, and inside it sat a brown owl, hooting softly. Three downy little baby owls with large round eyes were cuddled up next to her.

"Oh, aren't they lovely?" Rachel whispered to Kirsty as the mother and baby owls all blinked their big eyes at them. They didn't seem nervous, but the girls were careful to speak quietly and not startle them in any way. "But shouldn't *they* be asleep, too?"

"Yes, they should," Kirsty agreed. "Owls are only supposed to be awake at night."

Suddenly the girls heard the flapping of wings overhead. They glanced up and saw a snow-white owl, its feathers beautifully marked with silver, hovering just above the roof of the treehouse. As Kirsty looked a little closer, she saw that the owl's feathers were sparkling and glittering in the bright sunlight.

"Rachel, I think that's fairy magic!" Kirsty gasped, breathless with excitement as she pointed out the dazzling feathers.

"Are you a *magical* owl?" Rachel asked.

The snowy owl hooted softly and flapped her wings.

"I think she wants us to go with her!" Kirsty exclaimed.

Immediately the owl flew off the treehouse roof and circled above the girls. She shook her wings and a cloud of rainbow-coloured sparkles floated downwards, showering Rachel and Kirsty with fairy magic.

"We're becoming fairy-size, Kirsty!" Rachel laughed as she felt herself shrinking quickly down.

The mother and baby owls watched in astonishment as the girls turned into tiny fairies with gauzy, translucent wings on their backs. Then the snow-white owl shook her own wings again, and Rachel and Kirsty both shut their eyes as they were whirled away in a burst of magical fairy dust. Rachel's heart thumped with excitement as she wondered where the owl was taking them.

A few seconds later the girls opened their eyes to find themselves flying alongside the snowy owl over the familiar sights of Fairyland.

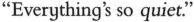

They could see the royal palace with
its four pink towers and the fairies' red
and white toadstool houses. But as they
swooped down, Rachel could tell that
something wasn't quite right.

"Isn't this strange, Kirsty?" she called.
"Everything's so *quiet*."

"I know," Kirsty
replied with a
frown.

"Oh!" Rachel
exclaimed suddenly
as they flew lower. "Now I can see *why*,
Kirsty. All the fairies are fast asleep!"

Kirsty realised that Rachel was right.
Everywhere the girls looked, they could
see sleeping fairies. Some were lying in
the meadow by the river, among the grass
and wildflowers.

Others were stretched out on the Fairyland beach in the sunshine. As Rachel and Kirsty flew past the toadstool houses, they peeked into the windows and saw fairies asleep in beds and in chairs. One had even fallen asleep while baking a cake in the kitchen.

There were also lots of fairies in the palace gardens. They were lying amongst the flowers, dozing peacefully, and one was even sleeping upright, leaning against a tree-trunk.

"This is all because of

Jack Frost!" Kirsty sighed. "Do you think we should wake the fairies up?"

"Let's see what the magical owl wants us to do," Rachel suggested.

The owl was just ahead of the girls, and she was hovering in mid-air, checking to make sure they were still following her. Rachel and Kirsty rushed to catch her up, and the owl led them to a tall tree in the middle of the palace gardens. There, nestled at the foot of a tree, the girls saw a fairy. She was fast asleep, just like the others.

"It's Yasmin the Night Owl Fairy!" Kirsty whispered to Rachel.

Snoring Goblins

The girls watched as the magical owl hooted gently, flapping her wings as she stared anxiously at Yasmin. But Yasmin didn't even stir. The owl began to hoot more loudly, batting her wings to and fro.

Whoo! Whoo! Whoo!

Suddenly Yasmin moved her head slightly. Rachel and Kirsty watched with relief as the fairy's eyes gradually flickered open and she yawned, wiggling her wings.

"Hello, Yasmin," Rachel said with a smile.

Yasmin's eyes now opened wide and she sat up. She wore a pink and white spotty T-shirt with a picture of an owl on it, cut-off denim shorts over pink leggings and sparkly pink trainers.

"Oh, Rachel and Kirsty, it's you!"

Yasmin exclaimed in surprise, flicking back her long dark hair. "I'm so pleased to see you. How did you get here?"

"A magical owl brought us!" Kirsty laughed, and the snowy owl hooted in agreement. Yasmin noticed the owl for the first time, and her face lit up.

"Shadow, you're *such* a clever bird!" Yasmin declared, glancing around the palace gardens at all the other sleeping fairies. "Girls, this is Shadow, a magical owl who lives in  Fairyland. She obviously realized that something was very wrong here, and went to fetch you."

"Something's very wrong in the human world, too, Yasmin," Rachel explained. "All the night-time animals are awake during the day, and all the day-time animals are asleep."

"And now all the fairies are asleep, too!" Kirsty added.

Yasmin shook her head in dismay. "This is all because my bag of magical sleep dust is missing," she sighed. "That's why everyone's sleep is topsy-turvy! Girls, will you help me get my bag back from those troublesome goblins?"

"Of course we will," Rachel said. Kirsty nodded in agreement, and Shadow the magical owl looked pleased and hooted with satisfaction.

"Then let's all return to Camp Stargaze right away!" Yasmin cried. And with one

flick of her wrist, a stream of shimmering
sparkles whirled from her wand and
surrounded them all,
including Shadow.

A few seconds
later they were
all back in the
Forest Fun
adventure
playground
just outside the
camp. Luckily
there was
no-one around.
Rachel and Kirsty

were still fairy-sized, although Shadow
was once again the same size as an
ordinary owl. She flew up into one of the
trees and settled there on a branch.

"Now, where are those naughty goblins?" Yasmin wondered. "I can sense they're around here *somewhere* with my bag of sleep dust."

The three friends began to search the playground. But as they did so, they

gradually became aware of a loud, rumbling noise above their heads.

"What is that noise?" Rachel asked, clapping her hands over her ears as it became louder. "It's awful!"

"It sounds like it's coming from the treehouse," Kirsty said, glancing upwards.

Yasmin nodded. "I think someone's snoring *very* loudly!" she said with a frown. "We'd better fly up there and check it out."

Rachel and Kirsty followed Yasmin up
to the treehouse, passing the owl's nest
on the way. The mother had gone to
hunt for food, and only the
three babies were
left, blinking their
huge eyes as
Yasmin and the
girls passed by.

Rachel, Kirsty
and Yasmin reached the
treehouse and peeped in through
one of the windows. They could hardly
believe what they saw. Four goblins were
inside the treehouse, curled up in different
positions under cosy duvets. They were
all fast asleep and snoring loudly.
"Perfect!" Kirsty whispered, trying not
to laugh.

"Now we'll have a chance to search for the magical bag."

"We'll have to be quick," Yasmin replied in a low voice. "If we don't find it, humans will be the next ones to start falling asleep while it's still daylight!"

Yasmin and the girls flew through the window into the treehouse. But as they did so, they heard a shrill, squeaky noise behind them.

Whoo! Whoo! WHOO!

Rachel spun round and saw the baby owls calling away in their nest, looking a little scared.

"Oh no!" Rachel groaned. "The baby owls must be frightened of the loud snoring, and they're calling for their mother."

"And now they've woken up the goblins!" Kirsty added in dismay as the goblins began to stir.

Topsy-Turvy

Rachel spotted the mother owl flying
back through the trees to comfort her
babies. But it was too late. The four
goblins were already awake, and they sat
up yawning and rubbing their eyes. They
all looked extremely annoyed.

"It's still day-time," one of them said
grumpily. "We're supposed to be asleep!"

At that moment the smallest goblin spotted Yasmin, Rachel and Kirsty hovering by the window.

"I bet *they* woke us up by making silly noises!" the smallest goblin screeched, pointing accusingly at them. "Horrible fairies!"

"Ignore them," ordered a long-nosed goblin. "We'll just go and find somewhere else to sleep until the sun sets. It's only a short time till then."

Still complaining loudly, the goblins began tucking their pillows under their arms and rolling up their duvets.

"It's silly sleeping in the day-time," the smallest goblin muttered sulkily. "We're *supposed* to go to sleep at night."

"Stop moaning!" snapped one of the other goblins, who had huge ears. "You know Jack Frost is having trouble sleeping, so he wants everyone else's sleep to be disturbed, too."

"And anyway," the long-nosed goblin added, grabbing his pillow, "If we sleep all day, that means we get to stay up and play all night long!"

Yasmin turned to Rachel and Kirsty. "I wonder why Jack Frost is having trouble getting to sleep?" she whispered. "Maybe that's why he hates the night-time so much."

The smallest goblin was still looking very sullen. "Well, *I'm* not sleeping very well either," he muttered. "You've all got lovely, cosy duvets, and mine isn't cosy at all!" He shot a jealous, sideways glance at the long-nosed goblin's duvet. "I want *that* one!" "No way!" the long-nosed goblin retorted.

But the small goblin grabbed a corner of the duvet and tried to pull it out of the other one's arms. The long-nosed goblin wrestled it away from him.

"I'll show you *exactly* how cosy this duvet is!" he yelled, and he grabbed the smallest goblin and began rolling him up inside it. The small goblin gave a shriek as he was left rolled up inside the duvet with just his head sticking out of one end and his feet sticking out of the other.

"And *I* got the flattest pillow," the goblin with the big ears grumbled loudly. "It's not fair. Everyone else's is *much* plumper than mine!" And he lunged forward, trying to steal the fourth goblin's pillow.

"Stop it!" the fourth goblin squealed, swinging the pillow at him and almost hitting Yasmin, Rachel and Kirsty. They just about managed to flutter out of the way in time, and instead he accidentally

hit the long-nosed goblin full in the face.

"Right! Now I'm *really* angry!" the long-nosed goblin howled. He grabbed his own pillow and began whacking the fourth goblin. Meanwhile, the smallest goblin managed to unroll himself from the duvet and began attacking the big-eared goblin.

Soon a huge pillow fight was in progress, and Yasmin and the girls had to keep flying around the treehouse to avoid being hit.

"I wonder where Yasmin's bag of sleep dust is?" Kirsty gasped as she dodged yet another pillow. "It must be here *somewhere.*"

"Just make sure you don't get hurt, girls," Yasmin told them anxiously as the big-eared goblin hurled his duvet over the smallest goblin, trapping him underneath. "The goblins will calm down soon, and then maybe we'll be able to find my magic bag."

Rachel nodded. It was then that she saw the long-nosed goblin sneaking over to the door of the treehouse.

The others hadn't noticed that he was sidling away while they carried on fighting and arguing. But Rachel could also see that he was clutching a goblin ragdoll.

Curious, Rachel flew down a little lower. The ragdoll was green, like the goblins, and it was wearing patched

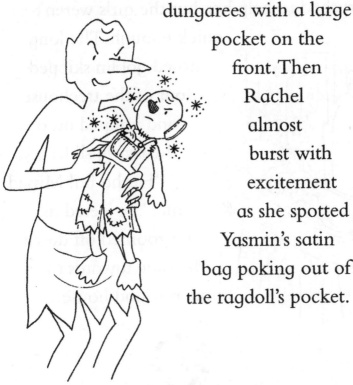

dungarees with a large pocket on the front. Then Rachel almost burst with excitement as she spotted Yasmin's satin bag poking out of the ragdoll's pocket.

"Kirsty!" Rachel called quickly. Her friend was closer to the door and the long-nosed goblin than she was. "Look at the ragdoll!"

Kirsty immediately glanced down and saw the doll the long-nosed goblin was holding. Her eyes widened and she swooped towards him to grab it. Rachel rushed to help her, but the girls weren't quick enough. The long-nosed goblin skipped out of the treehouse and jumped onto the twisty slide.

"Ha ha ha! Missed me!" he jeered as he zoomed off down the slide towards the underground house.

The other goblins rushed after him
and followed him down the slide. Yasmin,
Rachel and Kirsty flew after them, but
they couldn't catch them up. They were
just in time to see the smallest goblin
shoot into the underground house and
slam the door firmly shut behind him.

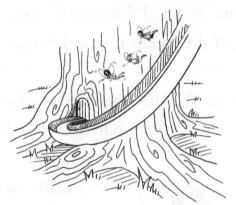

"What are we going to do now?"
Rachel panted, feeling very tired all of a
sudden. "The bag of sleep dust is hidden
in that ragdoll, but we can't get into the
underground house!"

"We'll have to wait until the goblins come out," Yasmin replied as they fluttered back to the treehouse "When it's dark, they'll wake up again."

Kirsty yawned widely. "I hope I can stay awake myself till then!" she remarked. "I suddenly feel really sleepy."

"Me, too." Rachel slumped down on the floor of the treehouse and began yawning, too.

"Oh dear!" Yasmin frowned, looking from Kirsty to Rachel. "Now Jack Frost's topsy-turvy sleep is affecting humans, just like I thought it would!"

"I'm sorry, Yasmin," Kirsty murmured, curling up on the floor next to Rachel. "But I'm just so sleepy."

"I can't keep my eyes open," Rachel whispered as she rested her head on her arm.

The last sounds the girls heard were the baby owls cheeping in their nest, still wide awake. And just a few seconds later, Rachel and Kirsty were both fast asleep.

Zip Slide Show!

"Oh!" Rachel opened her eyes and sat up. She blinked, trying to remember where she was. "What's that noise?"

Kirsty sat up too. "What's happening?" she asked in a dazed voice. Both she and Rachel were now back to their human size. "You fell asleep, girls." Yasmin was perched on the window ledge, smiling down at them.

"The sun set while you were asleep, and now it's dark, you've both woken up again. I made you human-sized again, just in case anyone came along and found you."

"But what *is* that noise?" asked Kirsty as they heard shouting and loud, stomping footsteps.

"The goblins are awake, and they're coming out to play!" Yasmin replied with a frown.

Rachel and Kirsty rushed over to the window and peered out of the treehouse. The playground was now lit up by a pale moon and a sky full of shining silver stars. Below them they could see the goblins rushing out of the underground house, yelling with delight.

"Yippee!" the smallest goblin shouted

gleefully. "It's night-time!"

Yasmin and the girls watched as the long-nosed goblin came out of the underground house behind the others. He was still carrying the ragdoll, but now it was in a pouch strapped to his chest like a baby.

"Here's the magic sleep dust!" the long-nosed goblin said proudly. He took Yasmin's bag from the ragdoll's pocket, opened it and sprinkled a generous handful of magical sleep dust into the air. It burst around the goblins in a shower of dazzling sparkles.

As Yasmin and the girls watched in
dismay, several grey squirrels suddenly
scurried past the treehouse. They were
bright-eyed and wide-awake as they

leapt from branch to branch.
"Those squirrels should
be asleep!" Yasmin
murmured, looking upset.
Meanwhile Rachel had
cocked her head to one side
and was listening hard.

"I can hear the cows mooing and the
sheep bleating in the distance," she said.
"They should be asleep, too."

"I can hear something else as well."
Kirsty pointed in the direction of the
campsite. "It sounds like people talking."

"Yes, people who should be getting
ready for bed by now!" Yasmin sighed.

"Jack Frost has got his wish. Everyone's sleep is topsy-turvy! Girls, we must get my bag back somehow, and fast."

"We need a plan," Kirsty said thoughtfully. She peered down at the goblins who were climbing up the ladders to the treetop walkways. "Maybe you should turn us into fairies again, Yasmin."

But Rachel shook her head. "No, I think I have an idea," she said. "You know how the goblins love to show off?"

Yasmin and Kirsty nodded.

"Well, maybe Kirsty and I can fool them into thinking we're scared of the adventure playground," Rachel explained. "Then, while they're showing off, Yasmin can fly down and grab her bag."

"Good idea!" Yasmin exclaimed.

Rachel and Kirsty hurried out of the treehouse. Yasmin followed, but remained hovering in the shadows out of sight.

"Be careful," Kirsty called to the goblins. "I nearly fell off one of those ladders."

"That's because you're not as clever and brave as we are!" the smallest goblin retorted, poking his tongue out at her. He rushed up the ladder and jumped onto the walkway where the girls were standing. Rachel gave a squeal as the walkway shook a little.

"Don't do *that!*" she exclaimed. "I don't like it."

Grinning, the goblin ran towards them. Giving little pretend squeaks of fear, Rachel and Kirsty ran along the walkway towards one of the other trees.

But then the big-eared goblin climbed up and blocked their way.

"Oh no, Rachel!" Kirsty wailed, winking secretly at her friend. "We'll have to cross the wobbly bridge to get away from them."

"But that's really scary!" Rachel complained.

All four of the goblins were laughing now as they chased the girls across the wobbly bridge.

"Go away!" Kirsty shouted.

"Scaredy-cats!" the long-nosed goblin sneered. He still had the ragdoll tucked firmly inside the pouch on his chest, Rachel noticed. "Why don't you have a go on the zip slide?"

"Oh, I couldn't do that!" Kirsty gasped in a frightened voice. "The seat whizzes along really fast."

"I'll show you how to do it!" the long-nosed goblin boasted. He climbed onto one of the zip slides and settled himself down in the seat. "Here goes!"

The goblin set off and whizzed confidently along the cable towards the opposite tree. As he did so, Kirsty saw Yasmin fly out of the shadows. The fairy swooped down from above the long-nosed goblin and made a grab for the bag in the ragdoll's pocket.

But the goblin spotted Yasmin immediately. He screamed with fury and clutched the ragdoll tightly to his chest with one hand while holding onto the zip slide with the other. Yasmin darted forward again and again, but there was no way she could pull the bag of sleep dust away from the goblin.

Kirsty and Rachel stared at each other in dismay.

"Yasmin can't get close enough to grab the bag!" Kirsty said. "What do we do *now*, Rachel?"

Shadow Swoops In

Before Rachel could reply, Shadow the owl suddenly came swooping down from the trees. She rushed towards the goblin, her magical white and silver feathers glittering in the pale moonlight as she flapped her wings and hooted loudly.

The long-nosed goblin looked terrified.

"Leave me alone!" he yelled, trying to shoo Shadow away with one hand and hold onto the zip slide *and* the ragdoll with the other.

Rachel saw her chance. She leapt onto the second zip slide which ran alongside the one the long-nosed goblin was travelling on, and zoomed off. Rachel was a long way behind the goblin, but Yasmin spotted her on the slide and guessed what she was up to. The fairy pointed her wand at the goblin and a burst of sparkling magic slowed his zip slide right down.

The goblin didn't notice because he
was so intent on fighting Shadow off. He
didn't even see Rachel whizzing towards
him. Rachel tensed as she got closer and
closer, her eyes fixed on the ragdoll's
pocket. Then, as she swept past the goblin,
Rachel reached out and grabbed for the
bag of sleep dust. But she ended
up pulling the ragdoll right
out of its pouch as she
zipped past.

"Well done, Rachel!"
Yasmin called. The
goblins, who were
waiting below for their
friend, had seen what had happened and
they groaned loudly. Meanwhile, Yasmin
flew over to Rachel and took her magical
bag from the ragdoll's pocket.

Still holding the ragdoll, Rachel reached
the bottom of the zip slide and jumped
off. Looking very sheepish, the long-nosed
goblin climbed off his zip slide, too.

"What's Jack Frost going to say, now
that the fairies have got the bag of magic
sleep dust back?" the smallest goblin

yelled at him.

"Oh, shut
up!" snapped
the long-nosed
goblin. "I'll tell
him it was all
your fault!"
Grumbling and
bickering, the goblins
trudged off through the trees. The long-
nosed goblin was last, dragging his duvet
with him and muttering under his breath.

Rachel ran after him and handed him
the ragdoll.

"Thanks!" the
goblin mumbled,
glaring at her.
Meanwhile,
Kirsty had
whizzed down
the twisty slide
from the treehouse to join Yasmin,
Rachel and Shadow.

"I can't hear the farm animals any
more," Kirsty said happily. "And the
camp's quiet now, too. Listen!"

They listened, but all they could hear
was the sound of the mother owl and her
babies hooting in their nest, and the rustle
of badgers snuffling around for food in
the undergrowth.

"Everything's back to normal!" Yasmin exclaimed happily. "Thanks to you, girls – and to Shadow, of course! Now I must rush back to Fairyland. Everyone will be awake now, and I can give them the good news."

Yasmin waved her wand and a mist of sparkles shrank Shadow down to her fairy size. Then, calling goodbye, Yasmin and Shadow flew off to Fairyland, their wings glowing against the dark night sky.

Quickly Rachel and Kirsty hurried back to their tent through the campsite where everyone was preparing for bed.

"I really thought we wouldn't be able to get the bag back from the goblin," Rachel whispered. "I'm so glad we did!"

Kirsty nodded. But as they reached their tent, both girls heard a very loud rumbling sound.

"My dad's already gone to sleep – and he's snoring!" Kirsty murmured to Rachel, trying not to laugh. "I wish I had a bit of Yasmin's magic sleep dust to stop him making so much noise, and then we could *all* have a peaceful night!"

Now Kirsty and Rachel must help...

Maisie the Moonbeam Fairy

Read on for a sneak peek...

It was a cool, dark evening and Kirsty Tate and Rachel Walker were standing with a group of children at the side of Mirror Lake – a wide, still expanse of water surrounded by hills. The two friends were staying with their families at a holiday park called Camp Stargaze and were having a wonderful week so far.

As its name suggested, Camp Stargaze was the perfect spot to see the night sky in all its glory, and there were lots of unusual and exciting activities for the campers to do every night. So far, Kirsty and Rachel had been to a campfire midnight feast, had gone firefly-spotting in Whispering Wood, and had studied the stars from the Camp's observatory... and tonight they were about to set sail for a moonlit boat ride!

"Come on then, you landlubbers," called Peter, the camp leader. He led them along a small wooden jetty, and Kirsty and Rachel saw that a motorboat was tied up there. "All aboard, me hearties!"

Chattering and laughing, the children clambered aboard. The boat was lit with lanterns, which sent golden reflections into the dark water of the lake. The boat rocked gently as people took their seats, and Kirsty squeezed Rachel's hand excitedly once they'd sat down. "Every time I go on a boat it reminds me of the first time we met," she said. "Do you remember?"

Rachel smiled at her. The two girls had met on a ferry one summer when their families were both going on holiday to Rainspell Island. Kirsty and Rachel had liked one another immediately, and had gone on to have the most amazingly magical time together that week – and lots more adventures ever since!

"Of course I remember," Rachel replied. "And I hope—" She broke off as Lucas and Matt, two boys that they'd made friends with, sat down nearby...

Read Maisie the Moonbeam Fairy to find out what adventures are in store for Kirsty and Rachel!

Meet the
Twilight Fairies

Kirsty and Rachel must rescue the Twilight Fairies' magical bags from Jack Frost or nobody will ever enjoy a night's rest again!

www.rainbowmagicbooks.co.uk

Meet the fairies, play games
and get sneak peeks at
the latest books!

www.rainbowmagicbooks.co.uk

There's fairy fun for everyone on
our wonderful website.
You'll find great activities, competitions, stories and
fairy profiles, and also a special newsletter.

Get 30% off all Rainbow Magic books at

www.rainbowmagicbooks.co.uk

Enter the code RAINBOW at the checkout.
Offer ends 31 December 2012.

Offer valid in United Kingdom and Republic of Ireland only.

Win Rainbow Magic Goodies!

There are lots of Rainbow Magic fairies, and we want to know
which one is your favourite! Send us a picture of her and tell
us in thirty words why she is your favourite and why you like
Rainbow Magic books. Each month we will put the entries into
a draw and select one winner to receive a Rainbow Magic
Sparkly T-shirt and Goody Bag!

Send your entry on a postcard to Rainbow Magic Competition,
Orchard Books, 338 Euston Road, London NW1 3BH.
Australian readers should email: childrens.books@hachette.com.au
New Zealand readers should write to Rainbow Magic Competition,
4 Whetu Place, Mairangi Bay, Auckland NZ.
Don't forget to include your name and address.
Only one entry per child.

Good luck!